**ANIMAL STARS**
Coco on the Catwalk

*Also in the Animal Stars series*

# ANIMAL STARS
# Coco on the Catwalk

Narinder Dhami

Illustrated by Strawberrie Donnelly

**Hodder
Children's
Books**

a division of Hodder Headline plc

**With thanks to Gill Raddings of Stunt Dogs
for reviewing the film and animal training information
within this book.**

First published in Great Britain in 1999
by Hodder Children's Books

A Catalogue record for this book is available from the British Library

ISBN 0 340 74403 0

Typeset by Avon Dataset Ltd, Bidford-on-Avon, Warks

Printed and bound in Great Britain by
The Guernsey Press Co. Ltd, Channel Isles

Hodder Children's Books
a division of Hodder Headline plc
338 Euston Road
London NW1 3BH

**1**

"I think Luke's in *lurve*!" Kim Miller giggled, as her older brother wandered dreamily out of the kitchen and just missed tripping over Harry, the Millers' Jack Russell, who was sitting in the doorway. Harry barked indignantly, but Luke didn't even notice.

"Do you really think so?" Sarah Ramsay, Kim's best mate, looked up from the magazine she was flipping through, her eyes wide. "How do you know?"

"Because he put his empty glass in the fridge, and the bottle of Coca-Cola in the dishwasher!" Kim pointed out, pulling the dishwasher open. Sure enough, there was a half-empty bottle of Coke sitting inside. Sarah began to laugh.

"You're right – he's out of it! D'you reckon he's got a girlfriend?"

"I don't know, but I'm going to make it my business to find out!" Kim grinned, as she poured two glasses of Coca-Cola. "Luke always tries to pretend he's not interested in girls, but I'm on to him!"

"I wonder who it is?" Sarah said, holding her hand out for one of the glasses. She and Kim had just got back from school and were having some tea. They were complete opposites to look at – Sarah was small and round-faced with short dark hair, while Kim was tall and slim, with long blonde hair. They weren't at all alike in personality either. Sarah was usually calm and controlled, while Kim had a temper that could raise the roof when she got going. Despite all that, they had been best friends for years.

Kim shrugged. "Who knows? Probably someone at his school." She opened the biscuit tin, and found some chocolate digestives. "Whoever she is, she must be crazy to fancy Luke – *if* she fancies him!"

"Oh, I don't know, he's not that bad," Sarah began, then she turned pink as Kim began to giggle. "For a *brother*, I mean!"

Harry and one of the Millers' other dogs, Spike, had smelt the chocolate biscuits, and were nosing eagerly round the girls' ankles. Spike, who was a shaggy mongrel with an incredibly appealing expression, began barking and pawing at Kim's shoes, while Harry, who was a bit more crafty, sat

up on his hindquarters and begged with his front paws held neatly out in front of him.

"OK, Harry, stop showing off!" Kim laughed. "You know you can't have chocolate – it's bad for you!"

Spike had sat up on his bottom now too, hoping that by copying Harry he might win Kim round.

Harry and Spike, and the Millers' other dog, Casper, a Golden Retriever, were all highly trained animals who had appeared on TV and in films. They'd been trained by Kim's parents who ran the *Animal Stars* agency, supplying animals for all kinds of media work. Apart from the family's three dogs, Kim's mother and father also had lots of other animals on their books, and could usually come up with whatever creature their clients desired, from cats to crocodiles. Kim loved being involved with *Animal Stars*, and she accompanied her parents on film and TV shoots whenever she was allowed to. She'd even starred in a commercial with Spike herself not long ago.

"When's your dad coming back from Scotland?" Sarah asked, reaching for another biscuit.

"Not till next weekend," Kim replied. Chris Miller was away on location at the moment with

Casper, who had a part in a TV series which was being shot in Scotland. Kim's parents occasionally had to work on jobs that meant staying away from home for a while, although they tried not to be away at the same time.

"So what're you doing tomorrow then?" Sarah finished off her Coke. "Do you want to come over to my house?"

Kim shook her head. "Sorry, I can't. Mum's taking Spike to the TV studios tomorrow, and I'm going with her."

"Oh, is Spike going to be in something else?" Sarah asked, looking interested. Spike hadn't lived with the Millers for very long, but his very first starring role in a soft drinks commercial had made him quite famous.

"Yeah, it's some kind of drama series about vets," Kim told her. "Mum's been teaching Spike how to limp!" She looked down at Spike, who was still waiting hopefully for a biscuit. "Paw stay, Spike!"

Spike immediately held up his paw as if it was injured, looking pathetically up at Kim and Sarah through the strands of golden-brown hair that flopped over his face. The girls laughed.

"He's so cute!" Sarah began, then a sudden loud buzzing noise made her jump. "What's that?" she gasped, looking round nervously.

Kim grinned as she pointed at the speaker on the wall. "I forgot to tell you – Dad's had an intercom fitted! He said he was fed up with yelling from the office all the time!" The *Animal Stars* agency was run from an office in a large room at the back of the Millers' house. "We've got one in here, one in the living-room and one upstairs."

"Wow, that's cool!" Sarah said, impressed.

"Hi, Mum," Kim called into the speaker. "What's up?"

"Oh, Kim, could you and Sarah come in here a minute?" Her mother's voice came through, sounding harassed. "I need some help stuffing envelopes!"

"OK." Kim turned to Sarah, who was already bouncing out of her seat. "You don't mind, do you?"

" 'Course not!" Sarah said eagerly. She was almost as interested in *Animal Stars* as Kim was.

The two girls went across the kitchen, and into the agency office. Kim's mother Rachel, who was only a few inches taller than Kim and had the same blonde hair as her daughter, was standing next to the filing cabinet, pulling out a folder. About twenty-five envelopes were heaped up in a large pile on her desk.

"Don't tell me!" Kim said with a grin. "Spike's fanmail!"

"Yes, and it's still coming in!" Kim's mother groaned, opening the folder which was marked *Spike's Publicity Photos*. "And we've had even more since the second *CoolCrush* commercial aired a few weeks ago."

"Hey, Kim, how much fanmail did *you* get then?" Sarah asked with a grin. Kim had appeared in the second commercial with Spike, and had enjoyed every minute of it.

"None!" Kim retorted, "But then I'm not quite as cute as Spike!"

"All the people who've written want pictures, so you and Sarah can put them into envelopes." Kim's mum took a fistful of photos out of the folder and put them on the desk. "I'll print off some copies of that standard letter we send out, and you can put those in too."

"OK. Oh, Mum . . ." Kim picked up the pile of envelopes from the desk. "Do you think

Luke's behaving a bit strangely?"

"Well, I noticed he had his shirt on inside-out when he left this morning!" her mother replied. "I didn't have time to tell him, so I don't know if he realised when he got to school."

"Well, *that* would've impressed the girl he's after!" Kim muttered to Sarah, and they both giggled. Kim's mum raised her eyebrows.

"Oh, so you think there's a girl involved, do you? Well, it was bound to happen some time." She stared hard at Kim. "I don't want you teasing the poor boy to within an inch of his life either, Kimberley Miller!"

"*Me*?" Kim began innocently, opening her blue eyes wide, but just then the phone on her mum's desk rang.

"Hello, *Animal Stars* agency," Rachel Miller said.

While Kim's mum was talking, Kim and Sarah stuffed photos into envelopes in silence, but a moment later the phone on Chris Miller's desk rang. Kim glanced at her mum, who nodded, so Kim went over to answer it.

"Hello, *Animal Stars*?"

"Allo?' Allo?" The woman's voice at the other

end sounded rather foreign and very agitated. "Who are *you*?"

"Er – I'm Kimberley Miller," Kim said politely. "My parents run the *Animal Stars* agency."

"Then let me speak to one of them immediately!" the voice demanded imperiously. Kim pulled a face, and glanced over at her mother who was just finishing her conversation.

"My mum's on the other line, but she'll be free in a moment," she said. "Who shall I say is calling?"

"Sasha Kinski." The woman paused as though she expected Kim to know who she was, then added "I am the personal assistant of Gianni Ricci."

Kim frowned. She knew *that* name but she couldn't remember where she'd heard it before.

"The fashion designer!" the woman told her impatiently. "Is your mother free now?"

"Er – yes," Kim muttered, and handed the receiver hastily to her mum. "It's Gianni Ricci's personal assistant!" she mouthed at her.

"Gianni Ricci?" Rachel Miller frowned.

"The fashion designer!" Kim hissed.

"Wow!" Sarah whispered, her eyes lighting up.

9

"Gianni Ricci – he's famous! Madonna wears his stuff!"

"And so do lots of film stars!" Kim whispered back. "I wonder what he wants with *Animal Stars*?"

They both looked over at Kim's mum, who was still talking to Sasha Kinski. "Yes, of course it's *possible*," Rachel Miller was saying. "In fact, I already have some pedigree cats on my books who would be perfect for the job. But I'd need to talk to Mr Ricci in a lot more detail first to find out exactly what his requirements are . . ."

"Sounds like Mr Ricci wants to hire some animals!" Kim said to Sarah in a low voice. "I wonder what for?"

"Maybe he wants to use them in one of his fashion shows!" Sarah suggested breathlessly.

"Yeah, cats on the catwalk!" Kim said, her eyes lighting up. She'd never been to a fashion show before, and this might be her big chance.

"Yes, I see," Rachel Miller was saying. "Well, I'm actually busy tomorrow, so maybe one day next week? Oh, I see. Right. Well, OK then . . ."

Kim's mum talked to Sasha Kinski for a few more minutes, and then she put the phone down. Kim was surprised to see that her mum looked rather dazed. Usually Rachel Miller was experienced enough to cope with anything.

"What's happening, Mum?"

"Well, it seems that Gianni Ricci is preparing for his London fashion show in a few weeks' time, and he's suddenly decided he wants his models to parade down the catwalk with cats on leads!" Kim's mum explained. "He wants me to find the cats, and train them for the show."

"Cool!" Kim and Sarah gasped together, their eyes wide.

"Yes, well, it's a bit short notice," Kim's mum said. "But they're going to pay very well indeed, so it would be stupid to turn it down!"

"Anyway, you've got lots of cats on the agency books who can walk on leads," Kim pointed out.

"Yes, but they'll all need to rehearse walking along the catwalk," her mum replied. "They'll be nervous because the runway is high up and they won't like being near the edge. And that's not all . . ."

"What?" Kim asked.

"Gianni Ricci wants his own Siamese cat Coco to be in the show," Kim's mum went on, "And she's not trained at all! So I've got a week or two to teach her how to walk on a lead."

"Oh, I hope I can meet Coco and come to the fashion show!" Kim said eagerly.

"Well, because we don't have much time, I've suggested that the cat comes here for two weeks' intensive training," her mother told her. "Mr Ricci's going to drive down with her tomorrow."

"Gianni Ricci's coming *here*!" Kim gasped, and nudged Sarah.

"Yes, so I'm going to have to ask one of the other handlers to take Spike to the TV studios," Kim's mum said, reaching for the phone. Because *Animal Stars* was getting so much work, Kim's parents couldn't cope with it all themselves, so they employed other animal handlers to do jobs for them when necessary.

Just then the door opened and Luke wandered in.

"Mum, have you seen my blue and black striped socks?"

His mum looked down at his feet. "You're wearing them."

Luke looked down too. "Oh, right," he said, and wandered out again.

"You'd better keep *him* away from Mr Ricci tomorrow, Mum!" Kim giggled, "Or he'll think we're all crazy!"

"Yes, and that's not all," Kim's mum muttered, tapping in the phone number. She grinned wryly as Kim and Sarah turned to stare at her. "It's just something that woman, Sasha Kinski, said . . ."

"What?" Kim asked.

"Oh, she made some remark about Coco," Rachel Miller replied. "Said the cat had to be treated carefully and considerately because it was very highly-strung . . ."

"Oh, yeah?" Kim glanced at Sarah. "Coco sounds like she's going to be a real character. I can't wait to meet her!"

**2**

"Hi, Kim!" Sarah rushed into the *Animal Stars* agency and did a couple of twirls. "Do I look OK?"

Kim, who was sitting in front of the office computer, glanced up from the screen, and looked Sarah briefly up and down. "Yeah, 'course you do. Why?"

"Well, it took me ages to decide what to put on this morning," Sarah replied, smoothing down her black and red dress. "I mean, what *do* you wear to meet a famous fashion designer?"

"Sarah, Gianni Ricci's clothes sell for hundreds of pounds," Kim pointed out. "I don't think he's going to be that impressed with a dress from Top Shop!"

Sarah grinned. "What're these?" she asked, pointing at a pile of photos next to the computer. The top one was of a long-haired white Persian cat with emerald-green eyes.

"Oh, those are some of the pedigree cats on *Animal Stars'* books," Kim told her. "Mr Ricci's going to look through the photos and choose the cats he wants for his fashion show."

Sarah glanced at the computer screen, where Kim was surfing the Net. "What're you looking for – stuff about Gianni Ricci?"

Kim shook her head. "No, I've been searching for websites about Siamese cats because I don't know that much about them." She hit the mouse a couple of times, and then nodded at the screen as a large photo of a pale fawn-coloured cat with brown face, ears, paws and tail gradually appeared. "Look, this is a Chocolate-Pointed Siamese. Isn't it gorgeous?"

"I don't know much about Siamese cats either," Sarah said. "What are they like?"

"It says here that they're affectionate, loyal and highly intelligent," Kim read out. "Self-assured and precocious."

Sarah looked puzzled. "Pre-what?"

"I think it means that they can be a bit spoilt, and like getting their own way!" Kim said with a grin.

"Well, let's hope Coco's not like that!" Sarah glanced at the clock. "When are they arriving?"

"Any minute now." Kim switched off the computer, and jumped to her feet. "Come on!"

The girls went out into the kitchen where Kim's mum was frantically rushing round tidying up, while Luke was sitting at the kitchen table, holding a piece of toast he wasn't eating and staring into space.

"Oh, Kim, put these in the dishwasher for me, will you?" Her mum thrust a pile of dirty plates into Kim's hands. "Luke, are you going to eat that piece of toast or not?"

Luke didn't answer.

"Mum said 'Are you going to eat that toast or not!' " Kim bawled in his ear.

Luke jumped. "No need to shout!" he snapped,

getting up to drop the toast in the bin. "I'm not deaf!"

"No, but you're daft!" Kim retorted, going over to the dishwasher. "Who is she, anyway?"

Luke turned a deep tomato-red. "I – I don't know what you're talking about," he stuttered.

"So why are you mooning around with a face like a wet lettuce then?" Kim demanded.

"I'm not!" Luke said crossly.

"You are!"

"That's enough, you two," Kim's mother broke in sternly. "Luke, take Harry out for his walk, will you?"

"Oh, *Mum*—" Luke began.

"*Now*, please."

Harry, who was looking a bit lonely now that Spike had gone off to the TV studios, heard the word "walk", and charged over to get his lead, which was hanging on the back of one of the kitchen chairs.

"Oh, all right," Luke grumbled, getting up and collecting his jacket from the hooks by the back door.

"Don't forget the dog!" Kim advised him as Luke reached for the door handle, and she and

Sarah fell about laughing. Luke turned pink, and hurried over to put Harry's lead on.

"I thought I told you not to tease him!" Rachel Miller said, raising her eyebrows at Kim as Luke and Harry went out.

"Oh, Mum, that's what brothers are *for*!" Kim pointed out with a grin. Secretly she couldn't help feeling a bit irritated that Luke was getting interested in girls. Even though they argued a lot, they'd always been pretty good mates. But now that Luke was getting older, they didn't seem to be so close anymore . . .

"Just don't wind him up about this girl, whoever she is," Kim's mum said, fixing her with a steely stare. Then the sound of a car pulling on to the drive at the front of the house made them all jump. "That must be them!" Rachel Miller hurried out of the kitchen, running her hands through her hair, and brushing crumbs of toast off her skirt. "Remember, you two – I want you on your best behaviour!"

Kim nudged Sarah. "Come on, let's go and see what's happening!"

The two girls hurried out of the kitchen and into the living-room. What they saw out of the large bay window made them both gasp. A huge, shiny black car had drawn up in front of the house, and a chauffeur in a pale grey uniform was opening the back door. As the girls watched, open-mouthed, a young woman with cropped blonde hair wearing a sharply-cut black suit climbed out.

Kim nudged Sarah. "That must be Sasha what's-her-name."

The woman was followed out of the car by an older man, who had long dark hair tied back in a ponytail, and who wore dark glasses and a cream suit.

"That's Gianni Ricci!" Sarah nudged Kim this time. "I've seen him on the telly."

As the fashion designer and his assistant walked up to the front door, the chauffeur leaned into the car and took out a large cat basket. Kim stared eagerly, hoping to catch a glimpse of Coco, but she couldn't see anything. So she and Sarah hurried over to the living-room door and peered curiously round it as Kim's mum was welcoming the visitors in.

"As you know, Mrs Miller, we don't have much time," Sasha Kinski was saying briskly, "So Mr Ricci would like to collect these photos you have for us, and get Coco settled in as soon as possible."

"Yes, she's feeling a little distressed after the drive from London," Gianni Ricci added in a heavily-accented voice as the chauffeur joined them with the cat basket.

Kim looked at the Siamese cat in its enormous basket, and thought that she'd never seen a *less* distressed animal in her life! Coco was sitting neatly and proudly on a red silk cushion with her paws tucked under her body and her long tail curled round herself. She wore an expensive-looking red satin collar studded with diamante,

and she looked very similar to the Siamese cat on the website that Kim and Sarah had been looking at, with her pale, beige-coloured coat and chocolate-brown markings. Her eyes were almond-shaped and a cool, clear blue, and she blinked lazily, looking completely in control of the situation.

"I have to say, Mrs Miller, that I'm still not completely happy about Coco moving in here with you." Gianni Ricci removed his sunglasses, and frowned. "Coco's very highly-strung, you see. She demands a lot of special care."

Coco yawned delicately and stared insolently at Kim and Sarah.

"As you want the cat trained so quickly, this really is the easiest way," Kim's mother said firmly. "You can tell us what Coco's routine is, and we promise we'll stick to it. Now if you'd like to come into the office . . ."

Gianni Ricci still looked unconvinced, but he nodded. Then, as Rachel led them down the hallway, he caught sight of Spike's rubber bone lying on the stairs.

"You have a *dog*?" The designer sounded so horrified that Kim almost giggled.

"Well, yes, three actually," Kim's mum told him. "But don't worry, Coco will be quite safe," she added hastily as Gianni Ricci looked as if he was going to faint on the spot. "We have a large cage for her, and an enclosed run in the garden."

"But Coco hates dogs – they upset her!" The designer looked quite upset himself. "She needs peace and quiet or she gets distressed. She's very timid, you know."

"I promise you, she'll be fine," Kim's mother reassured him, glancing over at the two girls hovering in the doorway. "Look, this is my daughter Kimberley and her friend Sarah. Why don't you leave Coco with them while we go into the office to talk? They can get to know each other."

Gianni Ricci stared suspiciously at the two girls. "They won't tease her, will they?" he demanded, "Because that upsets her!"

"Of course we won't tease her!" Kim said indignantly, ignoring the warning glance her mum gave her.

The chauffeur carried the basket into the living-room, and put it down on the carpet. Coco yawned again, and began to lick her paws.

"And don't let her out of the basket," Gianni Ricci added anxiously as Kim's mother ushered him out of the room. "And no loud music – loud noises make her nervous!"

"Is there anything that *doesn't* upset her?" Sarah muttered when Rachel had taken Gianni and Sasha to the office and the chauffeur had gone back to the car.

"Well, she looks fine to *me*." Kim knelt down and checked that the Siamese cat wasn't too distressed. "She doesn't seem the nervous type at all!" Coco was sitting with her eyes closed, ignoring them. "Hey, Coco." Kim pushed a finger through the wire mesh. "Hello there!"

Coco opened one slanting eye, stared at Kim for a second or two and then closed it again.

"What a madam!" Kim shrugged her shoulders. "She doesn't seem bothered about going somewhere new at all!"

By the time Kim's mother brought the designer and his assistant back into the living-room half an hour later, Coco was sleeping peacefully in her basket, and Kim and Sarah were watching TV, with the sound turned right down, of course, so that they didn't "upset" her.

"Daddy's come to say goodbye, baby," crooned Gianni Ricci, picking the basket up and holding it close to his face. "Say goodbye to Daddy, Coco!"

Coco immediately woke up and began to yowl piteously, pushing one of her soft, dark-brown paws through the wire mesh in an attempt to reach her owner. Kim grinned and nudged Sarah. "This cat's a real show-off!" she mouthed at her.

"Now you're sure you'll be able to stick to Coco's routine, Mrs Miller?" the designer asked anxiously. "Fresh chicken and fish *only*, anything else upsets her tummy, and she prefers to be fed by hand. She has to be kept in a quiet, peaceful place at all times, as loud noises make her nervous."

Coco responded to that with a blood-curdlingly loud miaow, and Kim and Sarah had to bite their lips to stop themselves from laughing.

"Coco will be fine, Mr Ricci," said Kim's mum patiently. "And if you want to come and visit her while she's staying here, just let us know."

"Thank you, Mrs Miller," said Sasha Kinski, who was beginning to look rather impatient. "We'll be in touch about the other cats we want to hire as soon as we've had a good look at the photos. Gianni, we *must* go."

Reluctantly the designer put the cat basket down, and went over to the door. "Oh, I nearly forgot!" he said suddenly. "I brought a few of Coco's things with me to help her settle in. I'll ask my chauffeur to get them."

They all went out, and Kim and Sarah followed them curiously. As Gianni and his assistant climbed into the car, the chauffeur staggered over to Kim's mother with a huge box in his arms.

"A *few* things!" Kim whispered to Sarah, as she glanced inside the box. "This cat's got more toys than I have!" The box was full of balls with bells inside, fur-covered mice and other stuffed toys, as well as a huge packet of cat treats from Harrods. There were also three more silk cushions and seven silver food bowls, each one engraved with a day of the week.

"The next few weeks are going to be fun!" Kim's mother groaned, closing the front door as the car drove off. "This cat sounds so nervous, I'm not sure I'll even be able to get it to come out of its basket, never mind walk on a lead!"

"She doesn't seem too bad," Kim began as they

all went back into the living-room. Then she stopped, and gave a gasp.

The cat basket was still in the middle of the room where they'd left it. But now the door stood wide open, and the basket was empty. Coco had vanished!

## 3

For a second or two they all stood and stared at the empty basket, too shocked to speak. Then Kim rushed forward and grabbed it.

"She's not here!" she gasped, pulling the cushion out as if she thought Coco might be hiding underneath it. "Where's she *gone*?"

Her mother and Sarah were already looking frantically round the room.

"What I want to know is how she got out in the first place!" Rachel Miller snapped, down on her hands and knees behind the sofa. "Kim, did you open that basket and not shut it again properly?"

"No, I didn't!" Kim said indignantly. "Mr Ricci told us not to let Coco out, and we didn't, did we, Sarah?"

"No, of course not!" Sarah agreed. "Maybe he accidentally knocked the catch open when he picked the basket up to say goodbye."

"Well, it doesn't really matter how it happened," Kim's mother muttered, looking pale and worried. "The point is, we've got to find her!"

They searched the living-room from top to bottom, but there was absolutely no sign of the Siamese cat. Then Kim had an idea.

"Maybe Coco sneaked out of the living-room while we were saying goodbye!" she suggested.

"Good idea!" her mum agreed. The three of them ran for the door, and hurried down the hallway to the kitchen. As they rushed in, Kim breathed a sigh of relief. Coco was standing by the dogs' bowls, wolfing down some food that Harry had left.

"Coco! You naughty girl!" Kim hurried over to her, and grabbed the bowl before Coco could finish it. "You'll be sick!"

Coco let out a loud yowl, and looked disgusted. Then she leapt lightly and gracefully up on to the kitchen table, and sat there swinging her tail disdainfully. Kim's mother groaned. "I don't know about this cat being nervous – but I've got a feeling *I'm* going to be a bag of nerves before too long!" She advanced on the Siamese cat, talking in a soothing voice. "Come here, Coco, there's a good girl."

"She doesn't *look* like a nervous cat, does she?" Sarah said doubtfully, as Coco watched Kim's mother coming towards her with an unblinking blue gaze.

"Nah, I reckon she's as tough as old boots!" Kim replied. Then, just as her mother reached out to pick the cat up, Coco jumped down off the table, and streaked out of the kitchen.

"Coco!" Kim's mother yelled anxiously. She, Kim and Sarah all rushed after her, and collided with each other in the doorway.

"Where did she go?" Kim gasped.

"Upstairs, I think," her mum replied grimly. "We'd better go after her. I don't want her running round on her own until I've had a chance to introduce her to the dogs, and settle her in."

29

The three of them crept silently up the stairs, listening hard, but they couldn't hear a sound.

"Kim, you look in your room and Sarah, you take Luke's room," Kim's mum whispered. "I'll check the bathroom and the other bedrooms."

Kim tiptoed along the landing to her bedroom. The door was slightly ajar, quite wide enough for a cat to have gone in there, so she pushed it open cautiously and went in. There weren't many places a cat could be hiding, so after Kim had looked under the bed and inside the wardrobe, she went over to the door again. Then a sudden movement on top of the wardrobe caught her attention.

"Coco!" she gasped. "How did you get up *there*?" The Siamese cat was sitting up on the wardrobe, amongst the boxes full of junk which were stored up there, swinging her tail from side to side and staring down at Kim with what looked like a very gleeful expression on her face. Coco had obviously jumped up on to Kim's dressing-table, and then leapt up on to the wardrobe.

"Come on, Coco!" Kim said gently, holding up her hand. "Come down, there's a good girl!"

Coco backed away from her, and yowled. Next

second, to her horror, Kim saw one of the boxes which were piled on top of the wardrobe teetering on the edge, then falling off. It was too late for Kim to jump out of the way and she was suddenly showered in old photographs, comics and bits of Lego.

"OW!" Kim roared as the lid of the box fell on her head. It was only made of cardboard and it hadn't really hurt her, but it was still a shock. Coco leapt down from the wardrobe, still miaowing crossly, just as footsteps were heard running along the landing.

"Kim, what's happened?" her mum called.

"Kim, are you all right?" Sarah shouted.

Just as they both reached Kim's room, Coco rushed out of the door, and down the stairs. Kim's mum and Sarah were both taken by surprise. Sarah tripped over the rug and landed flat on her front, while Kim's mum made a grab for Coco, missed and almost somersaulted along the landing. Kim couldn't help bursting into laughter.

"This is like something out of a comedy film!" she spluttered.

"Yes, well, I'm not laughing!" Kim's mum said grimly. "If that cat's nervous, I'll eat a whole packet of dog biscuits! I reckon she's *enjoying* all this!"

"There she is!" Sarah looked over the landing and pointed down the stairs. Coco was sitting on the bottom step, washing herself daintily. As Kim's mother started down the stairs, Coco glanced up, eyes narrowed.

"D'you think you'll catch her, Mum?" Kim asked in a low voice.

"I'm not even going to try," her mother whispered back. "We'll tempt her with some of those posh cat treats Mr Ricci brought with him!"

Coco waited on the bottom step, staring up at Mrs Miller, Kim and Sarah with a challenging gaze. Then, as they came within grabbing distance, the cat shot off towards the kitchen again.

"Kim, get the cat treats!" her mum told her, hurrying into the kitchen after Coco.

Kim grabbed the box, and ran into the kitchen. Coco had now squeezed herself behind the cooker, and was refusing to come out.

"Right, madam!" said Kim's mum, taking the box and shaking it loudly. "Look what we've got here. Lovely treats!" She reached under the worktop, and tipped some out on to the floor near the cooker. "Here you are, Coco."

They all waited silently for Coco to come out for the treats but nothing happened. The cat was refusing to budge.

"What about trying some dog food?" Kim suggested. "She seemed to like it before."

"All right," her mother agreed. "I'll try anything!"

So Kim put some food in Harry's bowl, and took it over. She placed it on the floor and, next second, an elegant, fawn-coloured head appeared round the side of the cooker. Then Coco pounced, and began gulping down the dog food as fast as she could.

"Got you!" Kim's mum gently took hold of Coco, and picked her up. The cat miaowed crossly, and struggled to get free. "Sarah, close the door," she said quickly, "And, Kim, get some of the cold chicken that Mr Ricci left for her out of the fridge. Once Coco realises that we're feeding her, I'm sure she'll settle in."

Kim quickly arranged some small pieces of chicken on a plate, and took them over to her mum. But when Coco was put down on the floor again, she showed no interest in the food her owner had provided for her. Instead she charged over to the bowl of dog food, and started scoffing it again.

Kim's mum groaned. "Coco, you're not supposed to be eating that!"

Coco ignored her.

"Oh, well, at least it's keeping her quiet!" Kim sighed.

"I thought Mr Ricci said that she couldn't eat anything except chicken and fish or it upsets her tummy," Sarah reminded them.

"Nothing's going to upset that one!" Kim's

mother said with a rueful smile. "Look at her, she's got us all running round in circles already! I've got a feeling that Madame Coco here is more than a bit spoilt . . ."

Right at that moment the back door opened unexpectedly, and Luke let Harry in, then walked in himself.

"Quick, shut the door!" Kim and Sarah shrieked together.

"And grab Harry!" Kim's mum yelled.

Too late. Harry, who wasn't on his lead, had instantly smelt the feline interloper in his kitchen. Not only that, it was eating from his bowl! Growling a little, deep in his throat, he advanced cautiously across the kitchen towards her.

Coco was still eating, but she paused and glanced up, staring at Harry with her brilliant blue eyes. She sat and waited, the tip of her dark tail swaying ever so slightly. Then as Harry got bolder and came closer, she leapt forward, spitting and hissing and arching her back as high as she could. Harry gave one single, scared bark, and scurried straight back across the kitchen to Kim.

"What a bully!" Kim said with a grin, as Coco

calmly returned to her bowl of dog food. "Poor old Harry – did she scare you?"

Harry whined and pawed at Kim's leg, wanting to be picked up so that he could examine this strange new creature in safety.

"I don't think we need worry about Coco and the dogs," Kim's mum said with a grin. "I think Coco can handle them!"

Luke was frowning.

"Where's that cat come from?" he asked in a puzzled voice.

"Oh, *Luke!*" Kim groaned. "It's Gianni Ricci's cat. He left it here to be trained!"

"I know *that*," Luke said sniffily. "Er – who's Gianni Ricci?"

"Luke," his mother remarked, "Do you ever listen to anything we say?"

"Not when he's in love!" Kim said wickedly, and Luke glared at her.

"Listen, we've all got to be careful from now on," said Kim's mother firmly. "I've got a nice big cage ready for Coco, but I don't want to keep her cooped up in it all the time, so no-one opens any doors or windows unless she's safely locked up, understand?"

Luke and Kim nodded, just as one of the agency phones began to ring.

"And someone had better make me a cup of tea," Rachel Miller added as she disappeared into the office. "I'm worn out chasing that cat all over the house!"

Luke shot out of the kitchen at speed and went up to his bedroom, so Kim went over to put the kettle on. Coco had licked Harry's bowl clean by now, and was sitting having a wash. But when Kim bent down to stroke her head, she shied away.

"She's not very friendly, is she?" Sarah asked, patting Harry who was sitting next to her and staring at Coco gloomily.

"I reckon she's sulking!" Kim said with a grin. "She probably hates having to leave her big, posh home, and coming to live here!"

"D'you think your mum will be able to train her?" Sarah asked doubtfully.

" 'Course she will!" Kim said confidently. "We'll be great mates, won't we, Coco?" she bent down to pat the cat again, and Coco stalked off, waving her tail elegantly.

"She doesn't *want* to be mates!" Sarah pointed out.

"Oh, she will!" Kim retorted.

"Bet you she won't!"

"Bet you she will!"

"OK, you're on!" Sarah held out her hand with a grin. "I bet you a pound you can't make friends with that crazy cat in one week!"

"Fine!" Kim held out her hand too. "Coco and me are going to be friends – you just wait and see!"

**4**

"Coco! What are you *doing*!" Kim dashed across the living-room, where Coco was happily shredding the magazine she hadn't read yet into strips with her sharp claws. "Give me that!"

Coco jumped up on to the arm of the sofa, looking disgusted, and miaowed at the top of her lungs. She had an expression on her face that said *you always have to spoil my fun!*

Kim looked sadly at a large poster of her favourite pop group which was scratched to bits.

"You're a right pain, you are!" she said, shaking her head. "How can I make friends with you if you keep being naughty?"

Coco didn't look at all bothered. Kim reached out tentatively to scratch her head, but the cat just wasn't interested.

"Why won't you be friends with me?" Kim asked crossly. "I'm quite nice, really!" Sarah had gone home earlier that afternoon and, before she'd left, she'd reminded Kim about their bet. Kim was determined to win it. If she was going to become an animal trainer like her parents, she had to learn to deal with difficult cases like Coco!

"Oh, she'll come round." Kim's mum came into the living-room, carrying a harness and a lead. "I think I'd better start training her right away. I was going to leave it for a couple of days until she's settled in, but she seems pretty much at home already! And we don't have a lot of time."

"What're you going to do?" Kim asked curiously.

"First of all, I'm just going to try and get her used to the harness." Rachel Miller put the harness and lead down on the floor, and then lifted Coco down on to the carpet too. "Hopefully that won't take too long."

"Aren't you going to put it on her?" Kim asked, as Coco began to sniff the harness delicately.

"No, not just yet," her mum replied. "Not till she's happy with it. Then in a few days' time we'll start using the lead too."

Coco batted the harness a few times, and when it didn't move, she lost interest. After a few minutes Kim's mum picked it up, and deftly fitted it around the cat's body. Coco didn't like that much. She began to howl loudly, and as soon as she was put down on the floor again, she rolled over and over, trying to pull the harness off.

"It's not hurting her, is it?" Kim asked anxiously.

"No, of course not," her mum replied, "She just doesn't like it because she's not in charge!"

Coco stopped rolling, and glared at Kim and her mother. Then she started trying to drag the harness off with her paw.

"We'll only leave it on for a few minutes today," said Kim's mum, glancing at the clock. "Kim, will you run upstairs and bring me one of the old blankets from the spare room? I want to make up a bed in Coco's cage for tonight."

Kim ran upstairs, and collected a blanket. On the way back across the landing, she happened to glance into her bedroom, and her heart sank. She'd brought a story that she was writing home from school on Friday so that she could finish it, and take it back for her teacher, Miss Walker, to mark. It was the longest story Kim had ever written – it was already ten pages, and still growing.

Kim had left the story on her desk, but now the papers were all over the floor. Kim rushed into her bedroom and snatched one of them up. It was crumpled and had claw marks in it, as well as several tears. Most of the other pieces of paper were the same too.

"*Coco*!" Kim said through gritted teeth, and ran downstairs. Her mum was just taking the harness off Coco and giving her a handful of cat treats, so that she would associate the harness with something good to eat. "Well done, Coco!" she was saying reassuringly, although Coco still looked mortally offended.

"Mum! Look what Coco's done to my story!" Kim wailed, holding the ruined papers up by one corner.

"Oh dear," Kim's mum looked upset.

"Shredding paper seems to be one of Coco's favourite things. You'd better not leave your work lying around from now on."

Coco miaowed, looking rather pleased with herself. She curled herself around Kim's mum's legs, and purred throatily in a very satisfied way.

"Don't you look at me like that!" Kim said crossily. "You and I are going to be friends, Coco, if it kills me!"

"Hi, how's Coco?" Sarah asked eagerly as she opened the Ramsays' front door to Kim on Monday morning. "Are you *bestest* friends yet?"

"No, we're not!" Kim groaned. "That cat shredded my story yesterday, and then she didn't like the cage Mum put her in, so she miaowed all night till Mum let her sleep on her bed!" She yawned and rubbed her eyes. "I didn't get any sleep at all!"

"I think this is going to be the easiest pound I ever earned!" Sarah said gleefully, slinging her school bag over her shoulder.

"I haven't given up yet!" Kim protested as they set off for Hightown Primary School. "Once Coco

43

gets to know me, we'll be mates – you just wait and see!"

"You don't sound too sure," Sarah pointed out with a grin, and Kim gave her a friendly shove. She didn't care that much about winning the bet, but she *did* want to make friends with Coco.

"How did Coco get on with Spike when he got back from the TV studios?" Sarah asked curiously.

"Just as well as she got on with Harry!" Kim replied. "Spike knows who's the boss now!"

Kim and Sarah were almost at the school gates, with just one more road to cross. Kim looked right and left, and was about to step off the kerb when Sarah caught her arm. "Watch it!" she hissed in Kim's ear. "Here comes you-know-who!"

A big white BMW car was tearing down the road towards the school, and going far too fast. It screeched to a halt, and the passenger door opened. Charlotte Appleby, who was in Kim's and Sarah's class, climbed out.

"Why does Charlotte's dad always drive so fast?" Kim muttered, as they crossed the road, keeping a sharp eye on the BMW.

"He always looks really bad-tempered too," Sarah whispered back.

"Bye, Dad. Bye, Annabel." Charlotte, tall and thin with jet-black hair, was waving at her father, and at her older sister, who was sitting in the back seat. A few seconds later Mr Appleby put the car into gear, reversed the length of the road and zoomed off.

Kim nudged Sarah. "Come on, let's go into the playground before Charlotte starts having a go at us!" Kim and Charlotte didn't get on at all. Not long ago Charlotte had almost got Kim into serious trouble by claiming that Kim had pushed her over and injured her arm, which wasn't true. Kim had nearly lost her chance to star in the *CoolCrush* commercial with Spike because of that, and since then she and Charlotte had given each other a wide berth.

As Charlotte followed them into the playground, Kim grinned at Sarah. "I bet Charlotte would be *wild* if she knew my mum was training Gianni Ricci's cat! You know how crazy about fashion she is!"

"Yeah . . ." Sarah glanced at Charlotte who had streaks of pink hair mascara in her black bob. "I bet Miss Walker tells her to wash *that* out when she gets home tonight!"

45

"I've just got to tell her about Coco!" Kim said eagerly. She didn't usually boast about *Animal Stars* and her parents' glamorous showbiz jobs at all, but there was something about Charlotte Appleby which got right up her nose. Charlotte was secretly jealous of Kim's involvement with *Animal Stars*, and she was always making fun of it or pretending she wasn't interested. "Come on, let's walk past her and Rosie and talk about it really loudly!"

Charlotte was chanting to her best friend, Rosie Randall, as Kim and Sarah strolled by.

"So your mum's training Gianni Ricci's cat!" Sarah said in a loud voice. "That must be really exciting!"

"Oh, it is!" Kim replied, with a sideways glance at Charlotte. "We met him on Saturday when he brought the cat to our house."

"D'you think you'll be allowed to go to the fashion show?" Sarah asked.

"I hope so!" Kim said, "That really *would* be exciting!"

"Your mum's training Gianni Ricci's cat!" Rosie Randall exclaimed, her eyes wide. Charlotte was frowning angrily, but Rosie didn't notice because she was a bit dozy. In fact, that was her nickname – Dozy Rosie. "Wow! Hey, Charlotte –" she dug her friend hard in the ribs "– did you hear *that*?"

"No," Charlotte said in a freezing tone, looking as if she'd swallowed a lemon.

"Kim's mum's training Gianni Ricci's cat!" Rosie repeated helpfully. Then she frowned. "But why does a footballer want his cat trained?"

Kim and Sarah burst out laughing. "Gianni Ricci's not a footballer!" Kim told her, "He's a fashion designer, and the cat's going to be in his show!"

"Oh, yeah, right." Rosie's frown cleared. "I was getting confused. Hey, Charlie!" She poked Charlotte in the ribs again. "You're interested in fashion, aren't you? You wanted to do a fashion page in the school magazine, but Miss Walker let Kim do her animal problems page instead!"

"I *know* that!" Charlotte said in a voice that dripped ice. Dozy Rosie finally realised that maybe she hadn't been very tactful, and her face dropped. Kim and Sarah hurried off, trying not to laugh too loudly, leaving Charlotte, hands on hips, telling Rosie off soundly.

"Oh, that was brilliant!" Kim chuckled. "Did you see Charlotte's face?"

"Yeah, but she would have been laughing herself if she'd seen you trying to cope with Coco yesterday!" Sarah said with a grin.

"I know, I know," Kim groaned. "But I'm going to make friends with Coco if it's the last thing I do! Come round to my house after school tonight and see how I get on."

"OK!" Sarah agreed eagerly, "I wouldn't miss this for anything!"

* * *

"Mum! What's going on?" Kim and Sarah had arrived at the Millers' house after school that afternoon, having popped in to see Sarah's mum on the way home. Now they walked into the Millers' living-room, and stared round at the mess in disbelief. It looked as if a bomb had hit it. The cushions were all over the floor, and a couple of pot plants had been knocked over, spilling compost everywhere.

"Coco was just letting me know how much she hates that harness I'm making her wear!" Rachel Miller sighed, climbing to her feet. "She's just not having any of it!"

"Where is she?" Kim asked, looking round.

"Behind the sofa, looking triumphant!" her mum sighed. "I've been praising her and giving her treats, but nothing seems to work. I've got a feeling she's so spoilt, that food rewards don't mean much." She grinned wryly. "And Gianni Ricci's phoned six times today to check on her – he even asked me if I could put Coco on the phone, so he could talk to her!"

Kim got down on her hands and knees, and looked behind the sofa. Coco, still wearing the harness, was sitting with her paws tucked neatly together in front of her, blinking lazily. She looked smug.

"Hi, Coco!" Kim said in a friendly voice, reaching out to scratch the soft fur on top of the cat's head. Coco let Kim stroke her for about two seconds and then retreated further behind the sofa.

"Look what I've got for you, Coco!" Kim went on. She and Sarah had stopped off at the pet shop near the school on their way home, and she'd bought a fluffy spider on a piece of elastic. She bounced it up and down in front of Coco, who stared at it disdainfully for a moment or two, but made no attempt to grab it.

Sarah giggled. "It's not working, Kim!"

"Come on, Coco." Kim's mum pulled the sofa aside so that she could reach the cat, and took the harness off. "Good girl!" she said, stroking her and giving her a piece of chicken. Coco sniffed it, and then ate it without showing much interest.

"She might think you're rewarding her for knocking the plants over, Mum!" Kim said with a grin. "Then she'll start doing it all the time!"

"Thanks a lot, Kim!" her mum groaned, and then gave an enormous yawn. "Sorry," she apologised, "But I didn't get much sleep last night with Coco trampling all over my head!"

"Are you going to try her in the cage again tonight?" Kim asked.

Her mum nodded. "If she won't settle though, I'll have to have her upstairs with me again."

"She could sleep on my bed," Kim offered hopefully. That might be a way of making friends with Coco, she thought.

"I don't think so," her mum replied. "You'll be falling asleep in class! Actually, I'll put her in the cage now, and see if she can get used to it. Then I've got work to do."

She carried Coco, who began protesting loudly, out of the living-room and into the kitchen. Kim and Sarah followed them. The cage, which was tall and spacious with plenty of room for some of Coco's toys and her litter tray, stood in one corner. Coco went into it rather gloomily, but she soon settled down on the old blanket Kim had folded into a bed for her, while Spike and Harry, who were lying on the kitchen rug together, kept a respectful distance.

"She seems OK now," Sarah said.

"Yes, it's at night she miaows the place down!" Kim told her.

Kim's mum was already heading into the office. "Help yourself to sandwiches or biscuits, girls," she called. "I'll make us a meal later on."

"You and Coco *still* didn't look too friendly, Kim," Sarah remarked with a wicked glint in her eye. "I expect you're wishing you hadn't made that bet with me!"'

"No, I'm not!" Kim retorted. Sarah grinned and went upstairs to the bathroom, while Kim began to make some sandwiches. She was just opening the fridge to get the cheese when Luke came in, and slung his schoolbag into the corner. The two dogs rushed to greet him, but he just patted them briefly without speaking.

"What's up with *you*?" Kim asked, wondering why he looked so depressed.

"Nothing," Luke muttered.

"Is it that girl?" Kim persisted.

"Just keep your nose out, Kim, all right?" Luke retorted.

"If you like her that much, why don't you just ask her out?" Kim went on, as she buttered slices of bread. She liked teasing Luke, but she didn't want him to be *unhappy*.

Luke shuffled his feet. "You don't

understand . . ." He shrugged miserably. "She's gorgeous . . . Loads of boys in my class want to go out with her. She wouldn't be interested in me – I've never ever spoken to her."

"Well, you won't know till you ask her, will you?" Kim told him.

Just then the phone in the hallway rang, and Luke went to answer it. Kim couldn't hear what he was saying, but a few minutes later he rushed back into the kitchen looking as if someone had just told him that he'd won a million pounds on the lottery.

"What's going on?" Kim began, but Luke hurried past her, stepping over the dogs, and charged into the *Animal Stars* office.

"Mum!" he gasped, "Is it OK if one of my – er – friends comes over now to do our homework together?"

"Yes, of course," his mum replied, staring hard at him. "Is it anyone special?"

Luke turned bright pink. "Er – yeah. I mean, no. Er – I think I'll go and wait outside for them."

"It was *her*, wasn't it!" Kim said gleefully as Luke rushed out of the office again. "That girl you fancy – I *told* you you should go for it!" But Luke was halfway to the front door, and didn't even hear her.

"What's going on?" Sarah asked as she came downstairs to find Kim running to meet her.

"The girl Luke fancies has just rung up and she's coming over!" Kim hissed, bundling Sarah back up the stairs. "If we go to my bedroom, we can see who it is!"

The two girls raced upstairs to Kim's room, and positioned themselves behind the net curtain, giggling.

"So she's really Luke's girlfriend then?" Sarah asked.

"Not yet," Kim replied. "He was just telling me that he didn't think she liked him, when she rang up and invited herself over – so she *must* fancy him!"

"Here they come!" Sarah said suddenly.

The two girls put their faces right up to the window and stared down the drive. Luke was walking back to the house, talking to a tall, very slim girl with long dark hair. She looked vaguely familiar.

"Oh no!" Kim gasped, clutching Sarah's arm.

It was Annabel Appleby, Charlotte's older sister.

## 5

Kim looked at Sarah, her face a complete picture of horror. Sarah's was nearly as bad.

"A-A-Annabel Appleby!" Kim stuttered. "It *can't* be her!"

"It *is* her!" Sarah took another peep out of the window. "How can Luke fancy *Charlotte's sister?*"

"And after what Charlotte did to me too!" Kim exclaimed furiously. "I nearly lost the *CoolCrush* commercial because of her!"

"What's Annabel like, anyway?" Sarah asked.

"I don't really know her."

"Nor me." Kim made for the door. "But she's Charlotte's sister, so she must be a horrible snob! I've got to tell Mum!"

"Kim, wait—" Sarah began. But Kim had already rushed off, her hot temper flaring up, as usual. She'd promised her parents that she'd try to control it in future, but the thought of her brother going out with *Charlotte's sister* was too much to bear.

"Mum!" Kim burst into the *Animal Stars* office, waking Coco up as she charged past and making her yowl crossly. "Mum, that girl Luke likes – it's Charlotte's sister!"

Her mother was working at the computer, and looked up, blinking. "What did you say, Kim?"

"That girl – it's Annabel Appleby!" Kim gasped. "You know, Charlotte's sister!"

"Oh, I see." Her mum shrugged. "Well, what's wrong with that?"

"*Mum*!" Kim could hardly believe her ears. "Charlotte nearly got me into big trouble, remember?"

"Yes, but that was nothing to do with her sister," Kim's mum pointed out reasonably.

"But, *Mum*—!" Kim could hardly get the words out, she was so angry. "If she's Charlotte's sister, she's bound to be horrible!"

"Oh, Kim, don't be silly," her mum snapped. "Now don't you dare embarrass Luke in front of Annabel. I want you to be on your best behaviour, understand?"

Kim opened her mouth to argue further, but her mum gave her a look which shut her up. She stomped out of the office and into the kitchen where Sarah was waiting for her.

"Mum says I've got to be *nice* to her!" Kim snorted in disgust as they heard Luke's key in the door. Then a nasty thought struck her. "What if they get *married*? I'll be Charlotte's sister-in-law!"

"Oh, Kim, don't be a prat!" Sarah hissed, "They're only fourteen!"

Luke, looking pink in the face and very pleased with himself, was ushering Annabel Appleby in through the front door. Kim had gone back to making sandwiches and was slicing cheese with a vengeance. She just couldn't understand it. How on earth could Luke fancy *Charlotte's sister*?

Luke was obviously trying to persuade Annabel to go into the living-room with him, but Annabel wouldn't. "I think I ought to say hello to your family first," Kim and Sarah heard her tell him.

Kim's hands were shaking so much, she was dropping most of the cheese on the floor, and Harry and Spike were hoovering it up enthusiastically. Whatever her mum had told her, she *was not* going to say hello to Annabel, Kim thought fiercely. Not after what Charlotte had done to her . . .

"Hi." Annabel Appleby walked into the kitchen, smiling widely. She looked very similar to Charlotte, but was rather more striking with her cat-like, slanting blue eyes and long dark lashes. "It's Kim, isn't it? And you must be Sarah."

"Er – hi," Sarah said, glancing at Kim. Kim kept her mouth shut tightly – until she saw her mum appear in the doorway of the *Animal Stars* office. Then she muttered a reluctant hello. Luke, who seemed too tongue-tied to introduce anyone to each other, was standing next to Annabel, shooting her adoring glances from time to time.

"Hello, Annabel," Kim's mum smiled, "I'm Rachel Miller. Nice to meet you."

"Nice to meet you too." Annabel bent down to fuss Spike and Harry who had hurried over to check out the new arrival. "And these two must be Spike and Harry. Aren't they gorgeous! I love dogs."

Sarah glanced at Kim again, and Kim frowned. She could tell what Sarah was thinking – *she doesn't seem so bad after all*! But Kim wasn't so easily convinced.

"Oh, wow, what a beautiful cat!" Annabel had just caught sight of Coco who was curled up asleep in her cage. "Luke, you didn't tell me you'd got a Siamese!"

"It's not ours," Luke said shyly, "It's Gianni Ricci's. My mum's training it."

"Gianni Ricci?" Annabel frowned. "That name sounds familiar."

"The fashion designer," Mrs Miller told her.

"Oh, yes!" Annabel looked excited. "Can I stroke her?"

Kim could see that her mum wasn't too keen, now that the troublesome Coco was fast asleep, but Luke was already unhooking the cage door.

"Of course you can," he said in a voice which implied that if Annabel wanted to *keep* Coco, he wouldn't say no.

"Be careful, she's not particularly friendly," his

mum began as Annabel reached in and stroked the cat's thick fur.

Rudely awakened, Coco leapt to her feet and miaowed in protest. Ignoring Annabel, she leapt out of the cage and looked round the kitchen. Meanwhile, Spike and Harry retreated into the agency office out of reach.

"Oh, she's lovely," Annabel breathed, as Coco jumped up on to the dresser, and sat there, eyeing everyone venomously. "Come on, puss!" She held out her hand but Coco ignored her, and Kim grinned at Sarah. For once, Coco had the right idea!

"Shall we go into the living-room?" Luke suggested, obviously longing to get Annabel to himself, but Annabel seemed quite happy where she was.

"By the way, Kim," she began, and Kim jumped, startled. She didn't want to talk to Annabel – what if she started going on about Charlotte? "I thought that *CoolCrush* commercial you did with Spike was brilliant!"

Kim was tongue-tied for a second or two. "Oh – er – thanks," she muttered at last.

"You were really good," Annabel added

# COCO ON THE CATWALK

enthusiastically. "Do you want to be an actress when you grow up?"

"Oh – no," Kim stammered as Annabel beamed at her, "I want to be an animal trainer too."

"Would you like something to eat, Annabel?" Rachel Miller asked, "Kim's just made some sandwiches."

"That'd be great," Annabel said, and sat down at the kitchen table.

"Luke, get some lemonade out of the fridge, will you?" Their mother went over to the sink. "I'll just make a quick salad."

Kim glanced over at Sarah. She could see that her friend was thinking exactly the same thing as she was. Annabel Appleby was actually *nice*. Or maybe she was just pretending ... Kim wasn't sure.

As Luke gave Annabel a glass of lemonade, Coco suddenly decided that she wasn't getting enough attention after all. She leapt lightly from the dresser on to the table, and began to step delicately round the plates and cutlery. Unfortunately, she knocked one of the glasses over, and a stream of lemonade cascaded all over Annabel's designer jeans. Kim watched with interest. If Annabel *was* only pretending to be nice, now was the time when she would show what she was *really* like!

"It's all right." Annabel jumped to her feet, and began brushing herself down. "No harm done."

"Coco, you idiot!" Luke said crossly, handing Annabel a huge wad of kitchen paper.

"Oh, it wasn't her fault," Annabel said quickly, mopping herself up. She was still smiling. "Pour me some more lemonade, Luke, would you?"

"Er – she seems nice," Sarah said cautiously to Kim later on as she put her coat on, ready to go home. After they'd eaten, Luke and Annabel had gone into the living-room and shut the door. They seemed to be getting on very well, judging by the sounds of talking and laughter which could be faintly heard.

"All right, so I was wrong!" Kim said ruefully. "Yeah, she seems OK. But I'm not looking forward to seeing Charlotte tomorrow!"

"What do you think *she'll* say about it all?" Sarah asked curiously.

"She's going to hate it," Kim replied, then she grinned. "Well, if it gets up Charlotte's nose, then I'm all for it!"

"Annabel seems nice, doesn't she?" Kim's mother said exactly the same thing as Sarah later that evening, when Kim was just about to go up to bed. Luke had gone up to his room earlier straight after Annabel had left, with a blissful look on his face. Apparently he and Annabel had a date at the burger bar after school tomorrow.

"All right, all right, don't go on about it!" Kim groaned. "I was wrong, OK?"

"Yes, so remember that in future." Her mother gave her a severe look. "And don't go jumping to conclusions about people!"

"I won't," Kim called over her shoulder, heading for the kitchen.

"Where are you going, young lady?" her mother said, going after her. "I thought I told you to get yourself off to bed!"

"I just want to say goodnight to Coco." Kim knelt down by the cage, and waggled her fingers through the wire mesh. Coco was lying on her blanket, but she wasn't asleep.

"I thought I'd try her in the cage again tonight," Kim's mum said. "If that won't work, she'll have to sleep in her basket – then *I* might get some sleep!"

"Come on, Coco – be friends with me!" Kim wailed, but Coco blinked lazily and didn't move.

"So slipping her bits of cheese under the table didn't help either!" remarked Rachel Miller tartly. "There must have been half a pound of Cheddar under there!"

Kim turned pink. "Sorry."

"Well, Harry and Spike gobbled it up anyway!" Her mum pointed down the hallway, hands on hips, "Now, bed!"

"I'm not going to give up, Coco!" Kim warned the cat, and went off up the stairs, yawning. Tomorrow she'd definitely think up some new ways to get along with that cat, or Sarah would win their bet . . .

Kim woke up in the darkness with a start. Her heart was thumping wildly. It was the second time she'd woken up. Coco had yowled so loudly around midnight, that Kim's mum had gone down, taken her out of the cage and brought her upstairs in her basket.

Then Kim remembered – she'd been dreaming that Charlotte had kidnapped Coco, and wouldn't give her back till Kim had promised to let her have her page in the school magazine . . .

A sudden loud, bleeping noise made Kim sit up. What was that? It sounded familiar. She swung her legs out of bed, and tiptoed to the door, which was ajar. Another loud noise made her jump, and then she realised where it was coming from. The speaker connected to the office intercom, which was fixed to the wall outside Kim's bedroom, was bleeping loudly.

Kim's blood ran cold. Burglars! Someone was in the office – someone who'd accidentally switched the intercom on, not knowing that there was a speaker upstairs . . .

At that moment Kim's mother and Luke both hurried out of their bedrooms.

"Mum!" Kim gasped, "There's someone in the—"

"Ssh!" Rachel Miller looked pale and anxious. "I know, I heard."

"Shall I call the police?" Luke whispered.

"I think you'd better," his mother said grimly. "Because whoever it is, they've got Coco. She was in my room in her basket, and now she's gone . . ."

## 6

Kim's heart almost stopped beating. Burglars had got hold of Gianni Ricci's cat? Or maybe they'd come to get Coco on purpose . . .

"Mum!" She tugged urgently at her mother's arms. "What if they know Coco's Mr Ricci's cat, and they want to kidnap her and hold her to ransom?"

"Kim, be quiet!" her mother hissed. "Go back to your room, and close the door. Luke, use the phone in my bedroom and call the police!"

Luke tiptoed across the landing, and Kim reluctantly turned to go into her bedroom. Then they all froze as more noises came over the speaker. A rustling and a scratching noise, followed by a familiar miaow.

"They've got Coco in the office!" Kim began, until Luke clapped a hand over her mouth.

"Who's there?" Rachel Miller said loudly into the speaker.

They all stood, holding their breath and listening hard for the sound of running footsteps. But they didn't hear anything. Except another miaow.

"I don't think there's anyone there," Kim's mum said, making for the stairs. "Except Coco."

"You mean they've gone, and left her behind?" Kim said, relieved.

"I've got a feeling there was *never* anyone there," her mother replied grimly, hurrying down to the hallway.

Kim didn't understand what she meant, so she followed her downstairs, and so did Luke. The office door was ajar, and Spike and Harry were sitting in the doorway, staring into the room. Kim's mother flipped the light switch on – and there was Coco, sitting on the intercom and pressing down the button which activated it. She blinked her big blue eyes in the sudden light, and let out a howl of protest.

"Coco!" Kim rushed over to her. "Are you all right?"

Coco allowed Kim to tickle her head for a few seconds. Then she stalked majestically over to the other side of the desk, and began attacking the telephone pad.

"So what happened to the burglars, Mum?" Luke asked, rubbing his eyes and yawning.

"Well, I'd better check all the doors and windows, but I don't think there *were* any burglars," his mother replied. "I've got a feeling that Coco here's to blame!"

"But how did she get out of her basket?" Kim began, then she gasped as she realised. "She must be able to undo the catch and open it – that's how she got out before!"

"And she decided to go for a midnight walk, and she ended up sitting on the intercom and frightening all us to death!" Luke finished. "Coco, you're a pain!"

Coco looked smug.

"Right, she'll have to go back into the cage then." Kim's mother reached out and scooped the cat up. "Come on, back to bed. We're never going to be able to get up in the morning!"

"I'm glad you weren't kidnapped, Coco!" Kim said, stroking the Siamese cat's thick fur. "Although I bet you'd have seen off any burglars single-handed, anyway!"

"Kim, I hope you're not going to yawn like that all day!" her mum said as she poured out glasses of orange juice the following morning. "Miss

Walker's going to think I let you stay up till all hours! And what *are* you doing?"

Kim was trying to eat toast with one hand, and open a pile of letters with the other. "I'm trying to sort out my page for the next school magazine," she said, through another enormous yawn. Kim's "animal problems" page in the *Hightown Herald* was proving very popular with the other pupils, who were always sending her letters asking for help with their pets.

"Well, hurry up or you'll be late," her mother told her, as she fed Spike and Harry. "Still, at least someone's catching up on their sleep!" She glanced at Coco who was snoozing happily in her cage, not moving a muscle.

Kim wasn't listening. She was intent on reading the letter she'd just opened. "Hey, this is great!" she announced when she'd finished. "It's just given me a brilliant idea!"

"What?" Her mother turned to stare at her.

"This letter!" Kim waved it in the air, as she jumped up from her chair. "It's from Shareena Sharma in Year 4."

"And?" Her mother looked puzzled.

"I'll tell you later!" Kim glanced over at Coco, as she grabbed her jacket and bag and dashed for the door. "I might have a surprise for you tonight, Coco . . ."

"So how're things going with Coco?" Sarah asked with a grin as she met up with Kim to walk to school.

"Oh, no different – and she nearly scared us all to death last night!" Kim gave Sarah a brief account of what had happened. "But I've got another cunning plan!"

"What?"

Kim pulled the envelope out of her pocket. "I've

had a letter from Shareena Sharma in Year 4, which has given me an idea."

"Shareena Sharma?" Sarah frowned. "I don't think I know her. What does the letter say?"

Kim shook her head. "I'm not telling you! But I reckon it might just help Coco and me to be friends."

Sarah snorted. "I'll believe that when I see it!" Then she nudged Kim. "Look, it's your future sister-in-law!"

Charlotte, who was walking to school for once, and Rosie Randall were just coming in through the school gates.

"Not funny, Sarah!" Kim gave her a push. "I wonder what she's going to say about Luke and Annabel?"

Charlotte had already spotted Kim and Sarah, and she had deliberately slowed down so they could catch her up. Kim guessed that Charlotte was spoiling for a fight because of Annabel going out with Luke, and she was ready for her!

"I suppose you know about my sister and your brother," Charlotte sneered. "Well, I think it stinks!"

"I don't – I think it's great!" Kim retorted. "They really like each other—"

"I don't know why," Charlotte broke in, "Annabel's really pretty, she can do loads better than *your* stupid brother!"

"Well, thanks goodness Annabel's nothing like *you*!" Kim glared at Charlotte. "And it was *her* who rang Luke up and asked to come over, so she *must* like him!"

An odd expression flitted across Charlotte's face so quickly, that Kim wasn't sure she hadn't imagined it. It puzzled her. Charlotte had looked almost – *pleased* . . .

"Come on, Rosie." Charlotte was already linking arms with her friend and turning away, before Kim had a chance to say anything else.

"Did you see that?" Kim asked Sarah.

"What?"

"That funny expression on Charlotte's face when I said that Annabel liked Luke," Kim said, still puzzled.

Sarah shrugged. "Oh, Charlotte's *always* got a funny expression on her face!"

Kim frowned. She was pretty sure she hadn't imagined it. But why on earth should Charlotte secretly be *pleased* that Annabel was going out with Luke? What was going on?

"Kim, what are you doing?" Kim's mum was taking the harness off Coco, who seemed to be getting quite used to it by now. Rachel had attached the lead to it today for the first time, letting it trail behind Coco as she walked around, and after a while, Coco had lost interest in it. "You're like a cat on hot bricks!"

"I told you, I'm waiting for someone." Kim hopped from one foot to the other in front of the window, as she stared down the drive. "Oh, here they are!"

"Who is it?" her mum asked curiously.

"It's Shareena Sharma from school." Kim waited till her mum had a firm hold on Coco, and then she rushed to open the front door. "And Prince William!"

"*Prince William?*" her mother repeated, bewildered.

"Hi, Shareena!" Kim opened the front door. "Thanks for coming."

"I told my mum to come back for me in an hour, is that OK?" Shareena said as she climbed out of the car. She was a small, slender girl with black hair cropped short.

"Fine." Kim waved at Mrs Sharma, who drove off, and ushered Shareena into the house.

"Hello, Shareena," Kim's mum began, and then stopped, surprised when she saw the cat basket in the girl's hand. "And who's this?"

"This is Prince William!" Shareena held the basket up, and a young Siamese cat with a beautiful, frosty-grey coat stared out at them. "He's a Lilac-Pointed Siamese."

"Shareena wrote to me because she thought Prince William was a bit lonely," Kim explained. "So she wanted to know if it would be a good idea to get another cat to keep him company."

"So you thought he and Coco might get along!" Her mother looked doubtfully at Coco who was sitting washing herself meticulously. "Hmm. Is Prince William fit and healthy, Shareena? And has he had his injections?"

Shareena nodded. Coco had already realised that there was another cat in the room, and was making her way towards the basket with an inquisitive look on her face.

"Don't get your cat out yet, Shareena," Kim

said hastily. She wasn't quite sure how Coco would react! She was hoping that the kitten would calm the older cat down and make her a bit more friendly. "Look, Coco, I've brought you a friend!"

Coco and Prince William sniffed cautiously at each other through the wire mesh. The kitten began to purr, looking interested, but Coco simply hissed and ran off. Then she jumped up on to the windowsill, and settled down for a nap. She didn't even show much interest when Shareena let Prince William out of his basket, and he padded around the room, exploring it. Instead, once she was sure she was safely out of the kitten's way, she simply went to sleep. Kim was disappointed. It looked very much as if Coco wasn't at all keen on having *any* friends.

"Thanks anyway, Shareena," Kim said as the younger girl carried the cat basket out to her mum's car an hour later. "Prince William's a lovely cat. I reckon you *should* get another kitten, because he definitely likes company."

"OK, thanks, Kim," said Shareena. "Sorry it didn't work out with Coco."

"Nothing's going to work with that cat!" Kim

said ruefully, as she stood on the doorstep and waved goodbye.

She turned to go back inside – and nearly fell over a blur of fawn and chocolate-coloured fur, which streaked past her at the speed of light.

"Coco!" Kim yelled, as the Siamese cat flew across the grass straight towards the large chestnut tree at the top of the drive. "Mum! Coco's got outside!"

Without waiting to see if her mother was coming or not, Kim dashed out into the front garden. She didn't know how the cat had got out – her mum had had to pop back into the office to get on with some paperwork, leaving Coco asleep on the windowsill, and Kim *knew* she'd closed the living-room door behind her when she came out to see Shareena and Prince William off. So how had the cat got out?

Coco had stopped and was sniffing the air curiously. Kim crept slowly up behind her, but Coco was on to her. She pelted away at the last minute, and shot up the trunk of the chestnut tree, clinging to the bark with her sharp claws. Then she hauled herself up on to one of the branches, and began to walk carefully along it.

"Coco! Please come down!" Kim called.

Suddenly Kim's heart was in her mouth as Coco missed her footing. The cat stumbled – and as she tried to right herself, her collar hooked itself over a stump on the branch which stuck out. Coco miaowed and tried to pull herself free, but she was trapped, and the next second she was struggling to breathe.

"COCO!" Kim yelled. If she didn't do something fast, the cat would choke to death!

**7**

Kim raced over to the chestnut tree. She didn't go in for climbing trees much now, but she'd been quite good at it when she was a bit younger, and she'd climbed the chestnut lots of times.

Coco was still struggling to free herself from the restriction round her neck, and her big blue eyes were full of panic. Her collar, expensive though it was, didn't have the usual elasticated section that would have allowed it to stretch so that the cat could get out easily.

"Easy, Coco." Kim tried to talk soothingly to the frightened cat as she climbed higher.

"Kim, why is the front door still open—" Suddenly Kim's mother appeared on the doorstep, and her eyes widened as she took in the scene in front of her. "Oh, my God!"

Kim was now inching along the branch where Coco was trapped. She reached out, struggling to lift the collar free of the stump, and after a few heart-stopping seconds she managed it.

Coco began coughing and miaowing all at once, and seemed thankful when Kim scooped her up with one hand. She clung to Kim with her pin-like claws, digging them through Kim's jumper and into her skin. It hurt, but Kim didn't care as she carefully made her way down the tree.

Kim's mother had stood silently by, her face pale and anxious until Kim and Coco were safely down again. Then she rushed over to them.

"Are you both all right? How did she get out?"

"I think she must be able to open the living-room door!" said Kim. She knew that cats could sometimes do that if the handle was the press-down type rather than a round knob, and they could leap high enough to reach it.

"This cat's a master of escape!" her mum said, shaking her head. "Are you *sure* you're all right?"

Kim nodded. Coco seemed to have recovered quite quickly too, but she was still clinging to Kim and purring loudly. When Kim's mum gently tried to take the cat herself, though, Coco miaowed, and dug her claws into Kim's jumper more firmly.

"Well, Kim," said her mum with a big smile, "I think Coco's changed her mind about you!"

"So we're friends now, aren't we, Coco?" Kim whispered, and kissed the top of the cat's head.

"This I've *got* to see!" Sarah announced as Kim unlocked the Millers' front door, and they walked in to be met by an excited Spike and Harry. It was the following day after school, and Sarah had insisted on coming home with Kim to see the transformation in Coco's behaviour for herself.

"You'd better believe it!" Kim grinned. "Coco let me put the harness and lead on her yesterday, no problem. I even walked her round the living-room. Then she sat on my lap all yesterday evening, and slept on my bed last night!"

Sarah groaned. "Sounds like I've lost the bet!"

"*And* she's started coming to me whenever I

call her!" Kim said proudly. She didn't add that that was partly because she always slipped Coco a small handful of dog food!

They went into the kitchen where Coco was fast asleep in her cage. The door to the *Animal Stars* office was closed, but they could hear Kim's mum talking on the phone.

"Hi, Coco." Kim tapped the cage, and Coco woke up, blinked and yawned. As soon as she recognised Kim, she leapt gracefully to her feet and began to purr, sidling along the side of the cage so that Kim could stroke her.

Sarah laughed. "OK, you win!" she said, flipping Kim a pound coin.

"Thanks!" Kim caught it neatly. "I'll buy us *both* some sweets with it!"

"Shall we go over those spellings for the test tomorrow?" Sarah suggested. "I still haven't got a clue how to spell half of them!"

"Yeah, OK." Kim agreed. She hit the button on the speaker, and waited for her mum's voice to come through. "Hi, Mum, me and Sarah are going to my room to do some homework. Can I take Coco with me?"

"I'm sure Coco'll be delighted!" her mum replied.

Just as Kim was lifting Coco, who was purring like a motor boat, out of her cage, the front door opened again, and Luke and Annabel came in, chatting animatedly. Sarah nudged Kim and winked.

"They're still going strong then!" she whispered.

Kim didn't get a chance to reply because right then Luke and Annabel came into the kitchen.

"Oh, hi," Annabel said with a friendly smile as the two dogs rushed over to greet her.

Kim and Sarah said hello, and then went out, Kim carrying Coco, who had snuggled down in her arms like a baby. As they went down the hallway, they heard Luke ask, "What do you want to drink, Annabel?"

"Oh, orange juice, please."

"Um – we haven't got any left," Luke replied anxiously. "We used it all up this morning."

There was a short pause, then he went on, "Well, I'll just bike over to the shop and get some then. Will you be all right here on your own?"

Sarah nudged Kim as they went up the stairs. "She's got him well-trained – a bit like Spike and Harry!"

"Yeah . . ." Kim frowned. "You know what? I

reckon there's something really weird going on."

"What do you mean?"

"Well, I know Charlotte's saying how much she hates Luke and Annabel dating, but she just looks so *smug*," Kim replied, as she put Coco down on the bed. "I noticed it at school again today. She just looks pretty pleased about something."

"It might not be anything to do with Luke and Annabel," Sarah pointed out, but Kim wasn't convinced.

"I'm sure it is – oh, hang on, I've left that list of spellings in my bag." She went over to the door again. "I'll go and get it – and you can entertain Coco!"

"Come here, Coco." Sarah held out her hand, but Coco moved out of her reach, a supremely superior expression on her face. "Obviously I've got to save her life first before she'll be friends with me!" Sarah added, pulling a face.

Kim laughed, and went out. As she was going along the landing, she heard the front door slam. Luke, going out on his shopping errand. Kim frowned again as she went slowly downstairs. Annabel certainly *seemed* very nice – so why did

she have this nagging feeling that something wasn't quite right?

"Get away from me, you stupid mutt!"

Kim froze just outside the kitchen door. That was Annabel's voice, full of irritation. Annabel was telling one of the dogs off, and in a low voice so that Kim's mum couldn't hear what she was saying from the office. But she'd said she *loved* dogs!

Puzzled, Kim pushed open the door, and

went in. Annabel was sitting at the kitchen table, reading a teenage magazine, and Spike and Harry had retreated over to the far side of the kitchen. Annabel obviously hadn't heard Kim coming down the stairs because now she jumped and thrust the magazine into her bag, with a very guilty look on her face.

"Sorry, I didn't mean to startle you," Kim said, going over to her bag which was next to Coco's cage.

"Oh, that's OK," said Annabel with her familiar wide smile. "Is it all right if I use the bathroom?"

"Sure." Kim shrugged, and Annabel went out. Kim waited till she heard the older girl's footsteps on the stairs, then she bent down to fuss Spike and Harry. "So why was Annabel telling you off?" she murmured gently. Maybe that was why Annabel had looked so guilty when Kim walked in – maybe she didn't really like dogs at all. Or maybe there was another reason . . .

Curiously Kim went over to Annabel's bag, which was still lying on the floor, and pulled out the magazine she'd been reading. Annabel had been so startled by Kim's sudden appearance, that she hadn't bothered to turn the magazine the right way out again, so it was still folded open at the page she'd been reading. The article was titled *How to become a model – we give you all the info you need*!

Kim stared at it for a moment or two. Then she pushed the magazine back into Annabel's bag, and rushed for the stairs. She took them two at a time, and then burst into her bedroom, startling both Sarah and Coco.

"What's up—" Sarah began, but Kim put her finger to her lips.

"Ssh!" She waited in silence until she heard Annabel open the bathroom door and go back downstairs again, and then she flung herself down on the bed next to Sarah.

"I've found out what's going on!" she gasped.

"What?" Sarah asked.

"Annabel's not really interested in Luke!" Kim announced furiously. "She wants to be a model – and I reckon she thinks that Luke can help her! *That's* why she's going out with him!"

Sarah frowned. "I don't get it."

Kim quickly explained how she'd heard Annabel being horrible to one of the dogs, and then about the article in the magazine. But Sarah still looked puzzled.

"Don't you *see*?" Kim went on impatiently. "Annabel thinks that because Mum's working for Gianni Ricci, maybe Luke will be able to get her a modelling job or something – or at least an audition!"

"Hang on a minute though, Kim." Sarah was trying to be the voice of reason like she always did. "Annabel couldn't have known about Gianni Ricci when she phoned Luke and came over that first time – remember?"

"She *said* she didn't," Kim pointed out grimly. "Luke couldn't have told her because he said he'd never even spoken to her. But there was *one* person . . ."

"Charlotte!" Sarah breathed, her eyes round.

"Yeah. That was the morning when I got up Charlotte's nose by going on about Gianni Ricci's cat!" Kim groaned. "And that was the afternoon when Annabel phoned Luke for the first time. Charlotte must've told her sister all about it when she got home!"

"So what're you going to do?" Sarah asked.

"Tell Luke, of course!" Kim retorted. "It's my

fault that he's getting conned like this. If only I hadn't gone on to Charlotte about Coco coming to stay ..."

# 8

"Er – Luke," Kim muttered diffidently, putting her head round her brother's bedroom door. "Can I talk to you for a minute?"

"What about?" Luke didn't look up from his computer screen. "I'm trying to do my homework."

"It won't take long." Kim went into the room and closed the door. Their mum was still in the office, working, but she didn't want to take the chance of being overheard. Although it was quite late in the evening, she'd had to wait until Annabel had gone home before tackling her brother.

Sarah hadn't thought it was a good idea at all, but Kim felt that she couldn't just sit back and do nothing. After all, it was all *her* fault that Annabel had found out about Gianni Ricci in the first place, and it was up to her to put things right. Anyway, she just couldn't bear the thought of Charlotte and her sister sitting at home laughing at them all.

"What do you want then?" Luke was still engrossed in his work.

Kim took a deep breath. "You really like Annabel, don't you?"

That got Luke's attention, and he looked up.

"Yeah, I suppose I do," he said suspiciously. "Why?"

"Well, do you think *she* likes *you*?" Kim went on.

"She's going out with me, isn't she?" Luke retorted. "Look, Kim, what're you going on about?"

"Um . . ." For once, Kim was at a loss for words. "I'm not sure Annabel *really* likes you . . ."

Luke was staring angrily at her. "Why not?"

"Well, I think she wants to be a model, and she knew about Gianni Ricci and Coco, and that's why she's going out with you!" Kim gabbled breathlessly.

The look on Luke's face showed her instantly that she'd made a big mistake. "*What* did you say?"

"It's true!" Kim said desperately. "I can prove it—"

Luke jumped to his feet, looking more furious than Kim had seen since she accidentally split lemonade on his compact disc player. "You're talking rubbish!"

"I'm not—"

"Get out!" Luke pointed at the door, his face white.

"But—"

"Didn't you hear what I said?"

Kim fled into her own bedroom, and shut the door. Coco, who was asleep on the duvet, sat up and began purring as Kim flung herself down beside her.

"He didn't believe me, Coco," Kim said sadly, scratching the Siamese cat under the chin. "So what am I going to do now?"

* * *

"Kim, what's going on between you and Luke?" Rachel Miller looked round from the dishwasher, where she was loading the dirty lunch plates. "You've both been in real moods since Wednesday. Have you had a row?"

"Sort of," muttered Kim, who was sitting at the kitchen table with Coco curled up on her lap. It was Saturday now, and she and Luke hadn't spoken a word to each other since they'd had that argument over Annabel. They were always falling out, but they usually made up pretty quickly. This time it was different though. And Luke was still seeing Annabel more often than ever. Kim just didn't know what to do. She'd thought about telling her mum, but she knew she would just tell her to keep her nose out. And after all, she didn't really have a lot of proof.

"Come on, cheer up," Kim's mum said briskly. "Your dad and Casper will be home next week. Tell you what – why don't we put Spike and Harry in the car, and take them for a walk down by the river? We can pick Sarah up on the way too, if you want."

"OK." Kim agreed listlessly, as Spike and Harry

sat up, tails wagging furiously at the word *walk*. At that moment one of the telephones in the *Animal Stars* office rang, and her mother went off to answer it. A second later the front door opened, and Luke and Annabel came in. Kim's heart began to pound. She'd tried to avoid Annabel ever since she'd rowed with Luke, but it wasn't easy. Annabel seemed to be round at the Millers' house all the time.

"Hi, Kim," Annabel said with a beaming smile. "How're you?"

"Fine," Kim muttered shortly. She could hardly bear to look at the older girl, and she kept her eyes fixed on the cat on her lap.

"Come on, Annabel, let's go and watch TV," Luke said urgently, obviously feeling almost as uncomfortable as Kim was.

"Oh no, I haven't said hello to your mum yet!" Annabel said firmly, and plonked herself down at the table next to Kim. It was all Kim could do to keep herself from getting up and leaving the room. If Coco hadn't been asleep so snugly on her lap, she would have done.

"Oh, hi, Annabel." Kim's mum came out of the office. "Guess what, Kim? That was Gianni Ricci."

Kim couldn't help glancing at Annabel, and she saw the way the other girl sat up eagerly. Luke, meanwhile, was fidgeting and clearing his throat.

"I told him that Coco's really getting used to the lead and harness now," Kim's mum went on, "There's going to be a rehearsal a week on Sunday with all the cats who are taking part in the fashion show, so that they can get used to the catwalk."

"How exciting!" Annabel breathed, and Kim shot her a deadly glare.

"I told Mr Ricci how well you and Coco are getting along, Kim." Her mum bent down and fondled the cat's ears. "Although I didn't tell him why! He was very pleased, and he's invited you to the rehearsal next week."

"Oh, Kim, aren't you lucky!" Annabel said enviously. She glanced at Rachel Miller. "I wish I could go!"

*Could you drop a hint that was any heavier?* Kim thought furiously. She glanced pointedly at Luke, but her brother was studying his fingernails with great interest.

"Well, if you really want to, Annabel . . ." Kim's

mum said slowly. "I suppose you can come with us. Though it won't be particularly interesting – the models won't be there for a start. This rehearsal's just for the cats."

"Oh, I don't mind!" Annabel's eyes were shining gleefully. "I'd *love* to come!"

"I'll have to check with Mr Ricci, when he rings me back next week." Kim's mum smiled. "But I should think it will be OK." She went over to the door. "I'm just going to get changed, Kim, then we'll go for that walk, all right?"

Kim nodded. She was trying not to look at Annabel, who was positively radiating smugness.

"Oh, Luke, I'm so excited!" Annabel announced. "It's really kind of your mum to take me!" She leapt up from her chair, disturbing Coco, who arched her back in a long stretch, and then jumped lazily down from Kim's lap. "Can I use your phone, Luke? I've just got to check with my parents that we're not doing anything next Sunday."

"Sure," Luke muttered. He ushered Annabel into the office, and Coco followed them, obviously thinking that something interesting was about to happen which she didn't want to miss. Kim sat tight, and waited for Luke to come out. She wanted to talk to him again. Surely he had to believe her *now* after what had just happened?

"See?" she hissed when Luke came out of the office and shut the door behind him. "I *told* you what she was after!"

"Oh, don't start that again!" Luke hissed back angrily.

"Well, it's obvious!" Kim snapped.

"Just because Annie's interested in fashion, it doesn't mean she's using me!" Luke retorted. "Now shut up about it, will you?"

A loud bleeping noise made them both jump. Kim and Luke looked round at the speaker on the wall, and next second they heard a voice coming through. Annabel's voice.

"– and then his mum invited me to go with her and Kim to the fashion show rehearsal next week!" Annabel was saying gleefully. "I'll get to meet Gianni Ricci – Charlotte, this is going to be my big chance!"

Kim glanced at Luke. "Coco must be sitting on the intercom again!" she mouthed at him, but Luke ignored her. He was concentrating fiercely on what Annabel was saying to her sister.

98

"And Luke doesn't suspect a thing!" Annabel continued in a self-satisfied tone. "And as soon as I've got to meet Gianni Ricci, I'll dump him!"

Kim couldn't help staring at Luke. He was looking so shocked that her heart went out to him.

"I've got a feeling Kim suspects something though," Annabel went on. "She's been behaving pretty strangely the last few days. I know – you think she's always strange!"

Kim glared at the speaker.

"I'll be home as soon as I can get away," Annabel yawned. "Luke's just so *boring*! Still, I got what I wanted!"

At that moment the sound was abruptly cut off, and Kim guessed that Coco had got bored with sitting on the intercom. Sure enough, a second or two later she could hear the cat scratching at the office door and whining. Silently Kim went over and let her out. She didn't say anything to Luke because she didn't know quite *what* to say. As she opened the door, Annabel was just replacing the receiver, still looking incredibly smug. Kim couldn't help smiling though, as Coco dashed out. Was Annabel in for a surprise!

"That's fine, Luke," Annabel said chattily as she

bounced back into the kitchen. "I can go next Sunday, no problem!"

"Oh, I don't think so," Luke said unsmilingly.

"Why not?" Annabel looked puzzled.

Kim took one look at her brother, and decided that he needed to sort this out for himself. "Come on, Coco," she said, scooping the Siamese into her arms. "Let's go upstairs."

She hurried out of the kitchen and shut the door. When she was halfway up the stairs, she stopped and gave the cat a big hug.

"Thanks, Coco," she whispered, "If it wasn't for

you, Annabel would have got away with it! You're such a clever cat!"

**9**

"Good girl, Coco!" Kim said encouragingly, as she and the Siamese walked the length of the hallway and back again. "You're really doing well!"

Coco was trotting docilely by Kim's side, lifting her paws elegantly, completely used to the harness and lead by now. Kim could hardly believe the change in the cat's behaviour. When she'd first arrived, she'd acted like a spoilt brat, but after almost two weeks of living with the Miller family, she'd changed almost beyond recognition. She'd even made cautious friends with Spike and Harry.

"You're doing brilliantly, Coco," Kim's mum called from the kitchen, where she was watching intently, along with the two dogs. "I really think we've cracked it, Kim – which is lucky, as the rehearsal's only a couple of days away!"

"I hope Coco's all right at the fashion show," Kim said anxiously, as she walked the Siamese back down the hall to the kitchen. "Won't it frighten her, being in front of all those people?"

"I don't think so," Kim's mum replied with a grin. "Coco's a big show-off. I think she'll enjoy it enormously!"

"I wish I could come to the fashion show," Kim said wistfully, as she bent down to take the harness off Coco, "And not just the rehearsal."

"Sorry, Kim," her mother said firmly. "I've done a fashion show before, when a designer wanted his models to parade down the catwalk with hawks and falcons on their wrists – and believe me, it's a nightmare backstage! There just wouldn't be any room for you."

"I could sit in the audience," Kim suggested.

Her mum shook her head. "Those places where they hold the shows are never big enough, and everyone's packed in like sardines as it is. There isn't room to swing a cat – sorry, Coco!"

"Oh, well, at least I get to go to the rehearsal," Kim said, as she fed Coco a piece of chicken. "Not like Annabel Appleby!"

"You know, I still can't believe that Annabel tried to use Luke like that," Kim's mum said angrily. Luke had told her what had happened a few days later. "Wait till I tell your dad when he and Casper get home tomorrow!"

"I know," Kim agreed, "Annabel turned out to be just as bad as Charlotte!"

"I think you and Charlotte should keep right away from each other from now on," Rachel Miller said firmly. "I mean it, Kim."

"All right," Kim nodded. But secretly she knew that if Charlotte ever got up her nose again, she'd *have* to fight back. She couldn't let Charlotte Appleby get one over on her.

"I hope Luke wasn't too badly hurt," Kim's mum went on. "He's been a bit quiet for the last week, but I suppose that's only to be expected."

The back door opened then, and Luke wandered in, a familiar, dreamy expression on his face. Spike and Harry immediately rushed over to greet him, but Luke barely seemed to notice.

"Hello, love," said his mum. "Are you all right?"

"What?" Luke blinked a few times, then smiled absently. "Yeah, I'm fine . . ." He put his bag down on the floor, went over to the fridge and took out a tub of butter. Then he wandered over to the cupboard, and got a glass.

"Er – Luke, I don't think you can drink butter!" Kim pointed out helpfully, trying not to laugh.

"Oh." Luke looked down at the butter and the glass. "I was going to make myself a drink and pour myself a sandwich." He frowned. "I mean—"

"We know what you mean!" His mum stood up. "Why don't you go and sit down and I'll do it for you."

"Thanks." Luke wandered out of the kitchen, looking as if his head was somewhere right up in the clouds. Kim and her mother smiled at each other with relief.

"He's in love again!" Kim whispered gleefully.

"Good," her mum whispered back. "That means he's over that awful Annabel Appleby!"

"Thanks to Coco." Kim bent down to pick Coco

up. The Siamese was obviously feeling neglected, and was winding herself sinuously in and out of Kim's ankles. "She really showed Annabel who's the boss!"

"Wow!" Kim breathed, looking round the decorated marquee, her eyes wide. "This is really cool!"

It was Sunday, the day of the fashion show rehearsal. Kim and her mother had been up bright and early, and Kim had groomed Coco, ready for her reunion with her owner. Then they'd made the short journey to London in the Millers' car, with Coco tucked away safely in her basket. Kim's mum had tied up the catch with a piece of string, just to be sure the Siamese didn't make another escape attempt on the way.

Gianni Ricci's show was only one of many fashion shows which were being held that week all over London in several different venues. But quite a few of the shows would be taking place in large marquees in the grounds of Hartington Palace, which was owned by one of the royal dukes. Kim had never seen the elegant, white house which was right in the middle of central

London before, and she was thrilled when her mother drove in through the big wrought-iron gates. There were security guards checking everyone who was coming in, and Kim had to have her own security pass, which made her feel very important.

Now they were inside the marquee where Gianni Ricci's show, amongst others, would be taking place next week, and the place was buzzing with activity. There were groups of men in overalls setting out rows of chairs along both sides of the catwalk, which stretched almost the whole length of the tent. At the top of the catwalk, on either side of the entrance where the models would first appear, there were two enormous, twisted trees with frosted silver branches that reached almost to the roof of the marquee, and two women were standing on stepladders, decorating them with bright white fairy lights.

"It looks pretty spectacular, doesn't it?" Kim's mum agreed. "You look after Coco, Kim. I'd better find Gianni Ricci and let him know we've arrived."

"No, no, no! This is not right!" Gianni Ricci was standing on the catwalk with Sasha Kinski and

another woman, waving his arms around in the air and looking harassed. "I've told you exactly what colour lipstick my models *must* wear! Get hold of it, even if you have to fly it in from the States!" Then his face suddenly lit up as he spotted Kim's mum. "Mrs Miller! And where is my Coco?"

"Over there with my daughter." Kim's mum pointed across the marquee.

Gianni Ricci rushed along the catwalk, and jumped down on to the grass. He nodded a greeting at Kim, then he grabbed the cat basket, and held it up. "Hello, my bambina!" he crooned, "Welcome home, Coco – I've missed you!"

Coco was obviously delighted to see her owner again. She jumped to her feet, miaowing a greeting, and began pressing her head against the wire mesh so he could tickle her. Gianni Ricci began to fumble impatiently with the catch, pulling off the piece of string and trying to get the door open so that he could take Coco out.

"Gianni, I need a word with you." Sasha Kinski hurried up to him. "In private."

"Thank you for looking after Coco so well," the designer said hastily to Kim as his assistant ushered him away, with the cat basket in his arms. "Enjoy the rehearsal."

"I will," Kim replied, feeling very sad that Coco wouldn't be coming home with them again afterwards. Although the Siamese had been difficult at first, she'd really enjoyed having the contrary cat to stay, and she hoped she'd have the chance to say goodbye properly when the rehearsal ended.

"Mrs Miller, where are those other cats?" Sasha Kinski called with a frown as she and Gianni climbed back on to the catwalk. "We need to start the rehearsal pretty soon."

"They'll be here," Kim's mum said confidently. There were nine other cats on the *Animal Stars* books who would be taking part in the fashion show, and they were all being brought along by their owners. "In fact –" Kim's mum glanced out of the marquee entrance "– I think I see some of them arriving now. I'll go to the car park and hurry them up." She glanced at Kim. "Sit down somewhere, love, and try not to get in the way."

Kim obediently sat down on a chair right in the front row and so close to the catwalk that she could touch it. Gianni Ricci and Sasha Kinski were standing talking, and the designer had put Coco's basket down near one of the enormous silver trees. The two women who'd been hanging the lights had finished, and were now folding up their stepladders.

Kim wondered what the *real* fashion show would be like when the marquee was crammed with people, the rich and the famous, newspaper journalists come to report on the latest trends and visitors from all over the world. It must be fantastic, she thought dreamily, wishing she could be there herself.

Kim was so busy daydreaming that she didn't notice Coco's paw snake through the wire mesh to fiddle with the catch on her basket. She hadn't noticed either that Gianni Ricci had taken off the string that Kim's mum had put on it to keep the basket securely closed. Suddenly the door of the basket flew open, and Coco trotted out, looking remarkably pleased with herself.

"Coco!" Kim gasped, jumping to her feet.

Gianni Ricci and his assistant looked round as they heard Kim's shout. At the same moment, Coco ran lightly across the catwalk and shot up the nearest tall silver tree.

**10**

"Coco!" Gianni Ricci wailed. He rushed over and stood staring tragically up into the branches, as Coco climbed higher. "Coco, come down! You'll fall!"

"What is that cat *doing*?" Sasha Kinski muttered, looking up at Coco with disgust. Then she had to jump smartly out of the way as a piece of silver branch broke off and almost fell on her head. "Gianni, she's ruining the trees and they cost a fortune!"

The designer took no notice of her. "Coco! Come back!"

Kim dragged her chair over to the catwalk, stood on it and climbed up. She could see that the branches of the tree were very brittle and guessed that they might not support the Siamese's weight for much longer. Coco might get badly hurt. And there was no way *she* could climb up to get the cat down, like she'd climbed the chestnut tree. There was only one thing she could try . . .

Kim raced up the catwalk and stopped underneath the tree where the designer and his assistant were already standing. Coco was still climbing purposefully, although twigs were snapping and cracking as she moved upwards.

"Coco!" Kim said in a firm voice.

Coco stopped, and looked down, clinging to one of the branches.

"Coco!" Kim said again, in an authoritative tone. "Come down!" And she put her hand in her pocket, hoping the cat would think she had some dog food in there.

Coco didn't move, and Kim held her breath. She was relying on the close relationship she'd built up with Coco over the last week or so, and the way the cat had responded to her before. Would it work?

Slowly Coco began to make her way down the tree, moving delicately from branch to branch. Gianni Ricci heaved a huge sigh of relief. He waited tensely until Coco was within reach, then he grabbed the Siamese and hugged her.

"Coco, you bad girl!"

"I'd better get someone to sweep this up," Sasha Kinski muttered, looking down disapprovingly at the bits of twig and silver glitter on the floor, and went off.

"Thank you!" Gianni Ricci was looking gratefully at Kim now. "Thank you very much – er—"

"Kim," Kim supplied helpfully.

"How did you get Coco to obey you like that?" the designer went on, hugging the cat closely to him. "She never listens to a word I say!"

"Oh, you just have to be firm with her," Kim said quickly, deciding she'd better not breathe a word about the dog food! "And by the way, Coco has worked out how to escape from her basket, so maybe you'd better get a new one."

"Oh, she's such a clever girl!" the designer said

fondly, kissing the top of the cat's head. Then he glanced at Kim. "And so are you! If it wasn't for you, Coco could have been badly hurt."

"Oh, it was nothing," Kim said modestly, reaching out to stroke Coco.

"I don't know how to thank you," Gianni Ricci went on. "Unless – would you like to come to my show?"

Kim's face lit up like a Christmas tree. "I'd love to!" she gasped.

The designer waved his hand airily. "Consider it done then. Oh, Mrs Miller –" he called as Kim's mum came back into the marquee with a group of people carrying cat baskets "– you have a very remarkable daughter!"

Kim couldn't help laughing at the surprised look on her mother's face. She could hardly believe her luck. She was going to see the *real* Gianni Ricci fashion show, *and* watch Coco parading down the catwalk!

Kim was so excited, she could hardly sit still on the seat which had been squeezed on to the end of the front row for her. Gianni Ricci's fashion show would be starting in the next five minutes. The marquee was packed with people, and Kim recognised quite a lot of them. There were several celebrities in the front row, including the Hollywood film star Melissa Murray, Alisha Kendall and Roxy Summers from the band *Golden Girls* and several television presenters. Looking round eagerly, Kim stored it all up to tell Sarah when she went home. She could see that quite a few of the audience were staring at her, wondering what she was doing there, but Kim didn't care.

The cats, including Coco, were all backstage, waiting for their big moment. Kim's mum had insisted that the cats had to have their own quiet place, away from the hustle and bustle of the models changing and being made up, and Kim hoped that all the animals had remained calm and unruffled. Especially Coco. She couldn't help feeling a little nervous about what the Siamese would do. Coco's behaviour wasn't exactly predictable!

The show began, and Kim sat forward eagerly in her chair.

"Please be good, Coco!" she prayed silently.

The cats didn't come on straightaway, but Kim didn't mind because she was spotting all the supermodels who were taking part, swaying languidly up and down the catwalk. There was Sindy Batista in a long green dress with glittering crystal embroidery that shimmered in the lights, Angelica Downes in the short lilac chiffon, Barbie Harris in the black velvet trouser suit and Danni Gordon in the pale pink shift dress. Kim had never seen anything quite as beautiful as the clothes they were wearing, and her eyes were out on stalks.

Then the first cat came out, with Sindy Batista. The supermodel was wearing a long, slinky white dress with a large spray of shocking pink flowers embroidered across the front, and the cat, who was a pure white Chinchilla called Morris, was wearing a shocking pink collar to match.

"Oh, that's lovely!" said the incredibly chic woman who was sitting next to Kim. Kim didn't know if she meant Morris or the dress, but Morris did look very cute indeed as he trotted placidly down the catwalk next to the famous model. The audience didn't seem to bother him at all, and Kim hoped fervently that Coco would be exactly the same.

The next model was Barbie Harris, and she had a Russian Blue called Ivan on a lead. Ivan's thick, blue-grey fur almost perfectly matched the pastel-blue shift dress and matching coat that Barbie was wearing. Kim knew that Coco would be next, and she crossed her fingers. She just hoped the Siamese wouldn't let them all down . . .

Angelica Downes, her long red hair swept up into a loose knot on top of her head, suddenly appeared at the top of the catwalk, with Coco next to her. Kim held her breath as Angelica walked elegantly forward, Coco trotting alongside her. Angelica was wearing a very striking two-piece suit in shades of fawn shading into seal-brown, which virtually matched the colours in Coco's coat, and the audience gasped, breaking into spontaneous applause. Coco looked round, obviously wondering what was going on.

"Go on, Coco," Kim muttered. "You can do it!"

Coco decided that she wasn't bothered by the applause – in fact, she liked it! She followed Angelica Downes down the catwalk, stepping lightly and delicately as if she'd been born to be a supermodel, and staring round at the audience with a superior look on her face.

"Well done, Coco!" Kim said under her breath, as the model and the cat paraded back down the

# COCO ON THE CATWALK

catwalk and the audience began applauding again. She felt very proud of Coco, but sad because after today she probably wouldn't see the cat again. But she'd never forget her – and she hoped that Coco wouldn't forget her either!

## MIDNIGHT THE MOVIE STAR
*Animal Stars 5*

Narinder Dhami

*When Kim Miller's parents start an agency training animals for TV and film work, she's delighted. She loves animals and she loves showbiz, and now Animal Stars is so busy, there's plenty of opportunity to help out . . .*

Animal Stars have been contracted for their first big budget movie: a legend about a mysterious black stallion. Midnight is perfect for the part! Visiting her mum on location, Kim befriends Caitlin, the daughter of the film's star, and, with Midnight's help, helps her overcome her fear of horses. But now Caitlin wants to go a step further and ride Midnight. Kim's not sure she's ready, but how can she say no to a movie star's daughter?

**TRIXIE'S MAGIC TRICK**
*Animal Stars 6*

Narinder Dhami

*When Kim Miller's parents start an agency training animals for TV and film work, she's delighted. She loves animals and she loves showbiz, and now Animal Stars is so busy, there's plenty of opportunity to help out . . .*

Famous magician, Richard Marvel, has asked Animal Stars to find him ten white rabbits for a trick in his next big show. There's only a short time to go, so Kim's mum has her work cut out for her, especially with naughty Trixie, the ringleader of the rabbits! Then the Millers get some shocking news. Richard has been accused of cruelty to animals. Kim's sure he's innocent, but can't prove it. Will the show go on?

# ORDER FORM

## *ANIMAL STARS* series
### *by Narinder Dhami*

| | | |
|---|---|---|
| 0 340 74400 6 | Animal Stars 1: Harry's Starring Role | £3.50 ❑ |
| 0 340 74401 4 | Animal Stars 2: Casper in the Spotlight | £3.50 ❑ |
| 0 340 74402 2 | Animal Stars 3: Spike's Secret | £3.50 ❑ |
| 0 340 74403 0 | Animal Stars 4: Coco on the Catwalk | £3.50 ❑ |
| 0 340 74404 9 | Animal Stars 5: Midnight the Movie Star | £3.50 ❑ |
| 0 340 74405 7 | Animal Stars 6: Trixie's Magic Trick | £3.50 ❑ |

*All Hodder Children's books are available at your local bookshop or newsagent, or can be ordered direct from the publisher. Just tick the titles you want and fill in the form below. Prices and availability subject to change without notice.*

Hodder Children's Books, Cash Sales Department, Bookpoint, 39 Milton Park, Abingdon, OXON, OX14 4TD, UK. If you have a credit card you may order by telephone – (01235) 831700.

Please enclose a cheque or postal order made payable to Bookpoint Ltd to the value of the cover price and allow the following for postage and packing:
UK & BFPO – £1.00 for the first book, 50p for the second book, and 30p for each additional book ordered up to a maximum charge of £3.00.
OVERSEAS & EIRE – £2.00 for the first book, £1.00 for the second book, and 50p for each additional book.

Name .................................................................................................

Address ..............................................................................................

...........................................................................................................

If you would prefer to pay by credit card, please complete:
Please debit my Visa/Access/Diner's Card/American Express (delete as applicable) card no:

| | | | | | | | | | | | | | | | | | | |
|---|---|---|---|---|---|---|---|---|---|---|---|---|---|---|---|---|---|---|
| | | | | | | | | | | | | | | | | | | |

Signature ...........................................................................

Expiry Date.........................................................................